This Walker book belongs to:

_____

_____

_____

To Gabriel, with love

First published 2017 by Walker Books Ltd, 87 Vauxhall Walk, London SE11 5HJ

This edition published 2019

2 4 6 8 10 9 7 5 3 1

© 2017 Petr Horáček

The right of Petr Horáček to be identified as author/illustrator of this work has been asserted
by him in accordance with the Copyright, Designs and Patents Act 1988

This book has been set in WBHoráček

Printed in China

British Library Cataloguing in Publication Data:
a catalogue record for this book is available from the British Library

ISBN 978-1-4063-8601-1
www.walker.co.uk

WALKER BOOKS
AND SUBSIDIARIES
LONDON • BOSTON • SYDNEY • AUCKLAND

Petr Horáček

The Mouse Who Wasn't Scared

One morning Little Mouse decided
to go exploring.
"Don't go and play in the woods,"
said Rabbit. "It's frightening
there and full of big, scary
animals."

"Nothing frightens me," said Little Mouse. "Not even big, scary animals. I may be small but I'm not scared of anything!"

Little Mouse walked deep into the woods. It was fun playing on the toadstools. Then she saw something curled up under the branches.

It was a wolf!
A BIG, SCARY WOLF!
"You don't scare me," said Little Mouse.
"Do you want to play?"

But the wolf
didn't answer.

Next Little Mouse played
hiding in the shadows,
when she saw something
sitting behind the tree.

It was a bear!
A HUGE, SCARY BEAR!
"You don't scare me!" said Little Mouse.
"Do you want to play?"

But the bear didn't answer.

Next Little Mouse played
jumping off a log, when
she saw something peeping
through the leaves.

It was a moose!
An ENORMOUS, SCARY MOOSE!
"You don't scare me," said Little Mouse.
"Do you want to play?"

But the moose stared silently.

"It's such fun playing here,"
said Little Mouse. "Rabbit was wrong.
The woods aren't scary - but no one wants
to play. Look, there's a little house!
I wonder who is inside."

Little Mouse crept up to the house.
What was that noise from
behind the door?

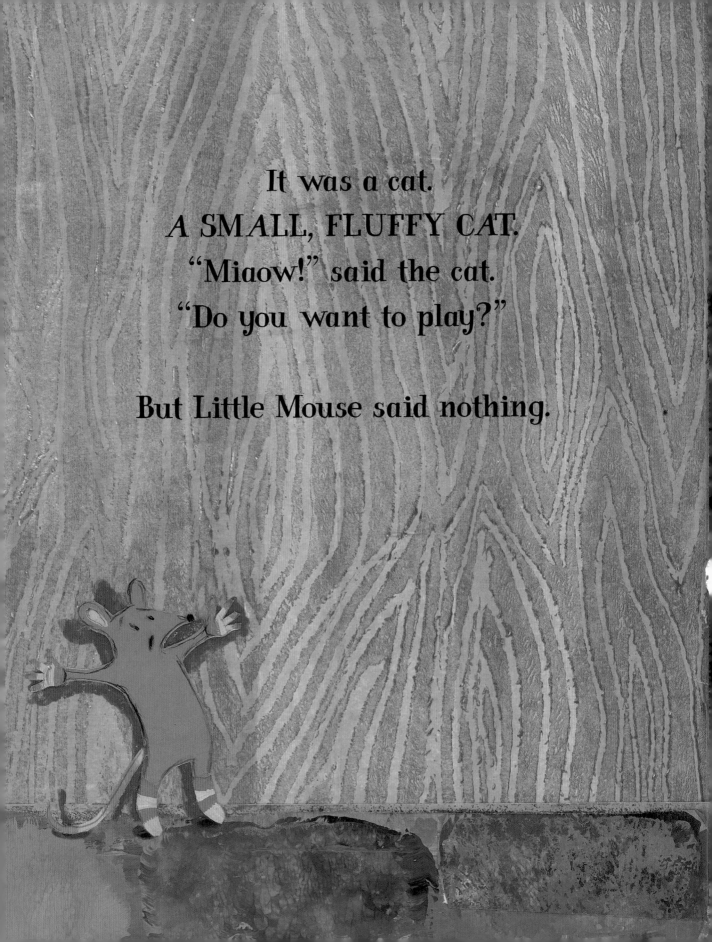

It was a cat.
A SMALL, FLUFFY CAT.
"Miaow!" said the cat.
"Do you want to play?"

But Little Mouse said nothing.

She ran out of the house ...

past the bear ...

past the moose ...

past the wolf ...

... all the way out of the woods.

"What's the matter, Little Mouse?"
said Rabbit. "Are you frightened
of the big, scary animals?"

"No!" said Little Mouse. "Big, scary animals don't frighten me. It's the small, fluffy ones that do!"

Also by Petr Horáček

978-1-4063-0122-9

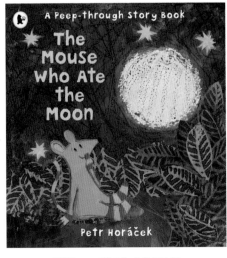

978-1-4063-6067-7

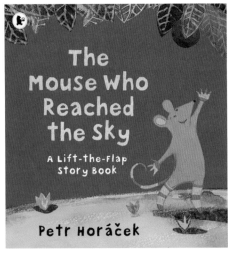

978-1-4063-6564-1

978-1-4063-3776-1

978-1-4063-6601-3

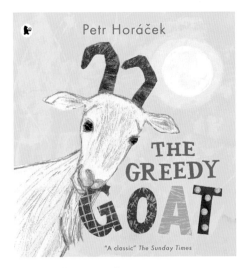

978-1-4063-7326-4

Available from all good booksellers

www.walker.co.uk